يِهْ – شِنْ

YEH-HSIEN

retold by Dawn Casey

illustrated by Richard Holland

Arabic translation by Wafa' Tarnowska

قيل في المخطوطاتِ الصِّينيِّةِ القَديمةِ إنهُ في قديمِ الزَّمانِ كانتْ فتاةٌ صغيرةٌ تعيشُ في جنوبِ البلادِ اسمُها يِهْ – شِنْ. حتى في صغرِها كانتْ ذكيةً ولطيفةً وعندَمَا كبُرَتْ أَصابَها حُزْنٌ شديدٌ إذ ماتتْ أُمُّها ثمَ ماتَ والدُها. بَقِيَتْ يِهْ – شِنْ تحتَ رعايةِ زوجةِ أبيها.

وكانَ لزَوْجَةِ الأَبِ ابنَةٌ من عندها فلَمْ تكُنْ في قَلْبِ الإمرأةِ أَيّةٌ محبّةٌ لِـ يِهْ – شِنْ كما لَمْ تكُنْ تُقَدِّمُ لها إلا فضَلاتُ الطَّعَامِ الْجافِّ ولمْ تُلبسْها إلا الألْبسةَ المُهَلْهَلَة. وكانتْ زَوْجَةُ الأبِ تَجْبُرُ يِهْ – شِنْ أنْ تجمعَ الحطبَ منْ أخطَرِ الغاباتِ وتَجْلِبَ الماءَ منْ أعمقِ البُحيراتِ.

وكَانَ لَدى يِهْ – شِنْ صَديقَةٌ واحدَةٌ...

Long ago in Southern China, so the old scrolls say, there lived a girl named Yeh-hsien. Even as a child she was clever and kind. As she grew up she knew great sorrow, for her mother died, and then her father too. Yeh-hsien was left in the care of her stepmother.

But the stepmother had a daughter of her own, and had no love for Yeh-hsien. She gave her hardly a scrap to eat and dressed her in nothing but tatters and rags. She forced Yeh-hsien to collect firewood from the most dangerous forests and draw water from the deepest pools.

Yeh-hsien had only one friend...

... وَهِيَ سَمَكَةٌ صَغِيرَةٌ ذَاتُ زَعَانِفَ حَمْرَاءَ وَعَيْنَيْنِ ذَهَبِيَّيْنِ. بَلْ كَانَتِ السَّمَكَةُ صَغِيرَةً عِنْدَمَا عَثَرَتْ يِهْ – شِنْ عَلَيْهَا إِلَى أَنَّهَا أَطْعَمَتِ السَّمَكَةَ طَعَامًا وَفِيرًا وَأَعْطَتْهَا حُبًّا حَنَانًا حَتَّى كَبُرَتِ السَّمَكَةُ وَأَصْبَحَ حَجْمُهَا ضَخْمًا.

عِنْدَمَا كَانَتْ يِهْ – شِنْ تَزُورُ الْبُحَيْرَةَ كَانَتِ السَّمَكَةُ تَرْفَعُ رَأْسَهَا فَوْقَ الْمَاءِ وَتُسْنِدُهُ عَلَى الشَّاطِئِ قُرْبَ يِهْ – شِنْ. وَمَا عَلِمَ أَحَدٌ بِهَذَا السِّرِّ إِلَى أَنْ جَاءَ يَوْمٌ وَسَأَلَتْ فِيهِ زَوْجَةُ أَبِي يِهْ – شِنْ ابْنَتَهَا:

"إِلَى أَيْنَ تَذْهَبُ يِهْ – شِنْ بِحَبَّاتِ الْأُرُزِّ هَذِهِ؟"

وَاقْتَرَحَتِ الِابْنَةُ: "لَوْ كُنْتِ تَلْحَقِينَ بِهَا لَعَلِمْتِ الْجَوَابَ."

اخْتَبَأَتْ زَوْجَةُ الْأَبِ وَرَاءَ عِيدَانِ الْقَصَبِ ثُمَّ انْتَظَرَتْ وَرَاقَبَتْ. وَلَمَّا رَأَتْ يِهْ – شِنْ تَارِكَةَ الْبُحَيْرَةَ ضَرَبَتِ الِامْرَأَةُ الْمَاءَ بِيَدِهَا وَرَشَّتْهَا وَهِيَ تُنَادِي بِنَغْمَةٍ نَاعِمَةٍ: "يَا سَمَكَةُ! يَا سَمَكَةُ!" لَكِنَّ السَّمَكَةَ لَبِثَتْ فِي قَعْرِ الْمَاءِ بِأَمَانٍ. فَشَتَمَتِ الِامْرَأَةُ: "أَيَّتُهَا أَحْقَرُ الْكَائِنَاتِ سَوْفَ أَقْبِضُ عَلَيْكِ..."

...a tiny fish with red fins and golden eyes. At least, he was tiny when Yeh-hsien first found him. But she nourished her fish with food and with love, and soon he grew to an enormous size. Whenever she visited his pond the fish always raised his head out of the water and rested it on the bank beside her. No one knew her secret. Until, one day, the stepmother asked her daughter, "Where does Yeh-hsien go with her grains of rice?"

"Why don't you follow her?" suggested the daughter, "and find out."

So, behind a clump of reeds, the stepmother waited and watched. When she saw Yeh-hsien leave, she thrust her hand into the pool and thrashed it about. "Fish! Oh fish!" she crooned. But the fish stayed safely underwater. "Wretched creature," the stepmother cursed. "I'll get you..."

في آخر النَّهار ذاتَ يومٍ قالَتْ زَوْجَةُ الأب لـ ـ يِهْ – شِنْ: "انَّك قَدْ إِشْتَغَلتِ جيِّدًا وتَستَحقيِّنَ فُستانًا جديدًا." ثُمَّ أجبرَتْ يِهْ – شِنْ أَنْ تُغيِّرَ ثيابَهَا المُهلْهَلةَ وأمرَتْ: "إذهبي الآنَ وإجلِبي الماءَ منَ النَّبعِ. لا تَستَعْجلِي بالعودَة."

ما إِن ذَهبَتْ يِهْ – شِنْ حتى لَبِسَتْ زَوْجَةُ أبيها فُستانَها المُهلْهَلَ وهرعَتْ إلى البحيرةِ. وكانَتْ تخبِّئُ في كُمِّهَا سِكِّينًا.

"Haven't you worked hard!" the stepmother said to Yeh-hsien later that day. "You deserve a new dress." And she made Yeh-hsien change out of her tattered old clothing. "Now, go and get water from the spring. No need to hurry back."

As soon as Yeh-hsien was gone, the stepmother pulled on the ragged dress, and hurried to the pond. Hidden up her sleeve she carried a knife.

رأت السَّمَكَةُ فُستانَ يِهْ – شِنْ وفي لَحْظَةٍ رفَعَتْ رأسَها خارجَ الماء. وفي اللَّحْظَةِ التَالِيَةِ طَعَنَتِ زَوْجَةُ الأبِ السَّمَكَةَ بالسكين. تخبَّطَتْ جُثَّةُ السمكةِ الضخمةُ حتى هَبَطَتْ على الضَّفَةِ خارجَ البُحَيْرَةِ مَيِّتَتًا.

قالتْ زوجةُ أبي يِهْ – شِنْ وهي تَطهُو السَّمَكَةَ وتُقَدِّمُها لِلعَشَاءِ: "لذيذٌ. إنَّ طعمَهَا ألَذُّ بكَثيرٍ مِنْ طَعْمِ السَّمَكِ العَادِيِّ." ثُمَّ أكلتْ المرأةُ وابنتُهَا حتى آخرَ لُقمةٍ مِنَ السَّمَكَةِ، صديقَةِ يِهْ – شِنْ.

The fish saw Yeh-hsien's dress and in a moment he raised his head out of the water. In the next the stepmother plunged in her dagger. The huge body flapped out of the pond and flopped onto the bank. Dead.

"Delicious," gloated the stepmother, as she cooked and served the flesh that night. "It tastes twice as good as an ordinary fish." And between them, the stepmother and her daughter ate up every last bit of Yeh-hsien's friend.

عِنْدَمَا نَادَتْ يِهْ – شِنْ سَمَكَتَها فِي الْيَوْمِ التَالِي لَمْ تَلْقَ جوابًا. وَلَمَّا نَادَتْ مرةً ثانيةً كانَ صوتُها غريبًا وعاليًا.

أَحَسَّتْ بِانْكِمَاشٍ فِي مَعِدَتِهَا وجَفَافٍ فِي فَمِهَا. رَكَعَتْ على رُكْبَتَيْهَا ويَدَيْهَا وأَخَذَتْ تُفَتِّشُ بينَ الطُّحْلُبِ، لكِنَّهَا لَمْ تَرَ شيئًا سِوَى البَحْصِ يَلْمَعُ فِي الشَّمْسِ. فَعَلِمَتْ أَنَّ صديقَتَها الوَحيدَةَ قَد اخْتَفَتْ.

أَخَذَتْ يِهْ – شِنْ تَبْكِي وَتَنْحَبُ وهِي منهارةٌ على الأرضِ ورأسُهَا مَدفونٌ بينَ يدَيْهَا. ولَمْ تَرَ الشَّيْخَ الْمُحَوِّمَ فِي السماءِ.

The next day, when Yeh-hsien called for her fish there was no answer. When she called again her voice came out strange and high. Her stomach felt tight. Her mouth was dry. On hands and knees Yeh-hsien parted the duckweed, but saw nothing but pebbles glinting in the sun. And she knew that her only friend was gone.

Weeping and wailing, poor Yeh-hsien crumpled to the ground and buried her head in her hands. So she did not notice the old man floating down from the sky.

أَحَسَّتْ يِهْ – شِنْ بِنَسمَةِ ريحٍ تَلمُسُ جَبِينَهَا. رَفَعَتْ عينيْهَا الحمراوينِ إلى الأعلى. نظَرَ الرَّجُلُ المسِنُّ إلى الأسفَلِ. كانَ شعرُهُ مُسدَلاً وثيابُهُ خشنَةً أمَّا عيناهُ فكانَتا مليئتيْنِ بالشفقَة.

قَالَ بِلُطْفٍ: "لا تبكِ، إنَّ زوجةَ أبيكِ قَدْ قتلَتْ سمكتَكِ وخبَّأَتْ الحَسَكَ في كومةِ السَّمادِ. إذهَبِي وإجلِبِي الحَسَكَ. إنَّ فيهِ سحرًا قويًا يُلبِّي كُلَّ ما تَتَمَنَّينَهُ."

A breath of wind touched her brow, and with reddened eyes Yeh-hsien looked up. The old man looked down. His hair was loose and his clothes were coarse but his eyes were full of compassion.

"Don't cry," he said gently. "Your stepmother killed your fish and hid the bones in the dung heap. Go, fetch the fish bones. They contain powerful magic. Whatever you wish for, they will grant it."

سمِعَتْ يِهْ – شِنْ كلامَ الرَّجُلِ الحكيمِ وخبَّأَتِ الحسَكَ في غُرْفتهَا. وكانتْ تُخرِجُهُ أحيانًا كثيرةً مِنْ مخبئَهِ وتَمْسِكُهُ فتَشْعُرُ ببرودَتِهِ ونُعومَتِهِ وثِقَلِهِ في يَدَيهَا. أكثَرُ الأحيانِ كانتْ تَتَذكَّرُ صديقتَهَا، وبعضُ الأحيانِ كانتْ تتمنَّى أُمنيةً.

فأصبَحَ لدى يِهْ – شِنِ كُلُّ ما كانتْ تحتاجُهُ مِنَ الطَّعامِ والملابسِ واليَشَمِ الثمينِ ولآلئَ مِنْ لَوْنِ القمَرِ.

Yeh-hsien followed the wise man's advice and hid the fish bones in her room. She would often take them out and hold them. They felt smooth and cool and heavy in her hands. Mostly, she remembered her friend. But sometimes, she made a wish.

Now Yeh-hsien had all the food and clothes she needed, as well as precious jade and moon-pale pearls.

جاءَ فصلُ الرَّبيعِ تُعلِنُ قدومَهُ رائحةُ زهْرِ شجَرِ الخَوْخِ.

وحانَ وقتُ مهرجانِ الربيعِ، حيثُ يجتمعُ الناسُ لتكريمِ أجدادِهِمْ، وحيثُ يتمنَّى الشبانُ والشاباتُ أَنْ يَلْقَوْا على أزواجٍ وزوجاتٍ.

تنهَّدَتْ يِهْ – شِنْ: "آهِ، كَمْ أَتمَنَّى أَنْ أَحْضُرَ المَهْرجانَ."

Soon the scent of plum blossom announced the arrival of spring. It was time for the Spring Festival, where people gathered to honour their ancestors and young women and men hoped to find husbands and wives.
"Oh, how I would love to go," Yeh-hsien sighed.

قالَت ابْنَةُ زوجَةِ أبي يِهْ – شِنْ: "أنتِ؟! لا يُمكنُكِ حُضور المهرجان!"

نَهَرَتْهَا زوجةُ الأب: "يَجبُ أَن تَبْقَيْ هُنَا ناطورةَ على أشجارِ الفاكِهَة."

وهكذا كانَ الأمرُ، أو كادَ أَنْ يكونَ لو لَمْ تكُنْ يِهْ – شِنْ مُصَمِّمَةً على أَنْ تَحْضُرَ.

"You?!" said the stepsister. "You can't go!"

"*You* must stay and guard the fruit trees," ordered the stepmother.

So that was that. Or it would have been if Yeh-hsien had not been so determined.

عِنْدَمَا ذهبَتْ زوجةُ أبيها وابنتُها ركعَتْ يِهْ – شِنْ أَمَامَ حَسَكِ السَّمَكة وتَمَنَّتْ أُمنِيةً تَلَبَّتْ بثانِيةٍ واحدةٍ.

أَصْبَحَتْ يِهْ – شِنْ لابِسةً فُستانًا مِنَ الحرير ومِعْطَفًا مصنوعًا من ريشِ طائرِ القاوَنْدْ. كُلُّ ريشةٍ فيه ساطعةٌ تَبْهَرُ البَصَرَ. كُلَّمَا تحَرَّكَتْ يِهْ – شِنْ لَمَعَتْ كُلُّ ريشَةٍ بجميعِ أطيافِ اللَّونِ الأزرَقِ المُمْكِنة ومنها الأزرَقِ النيليِّ اللازوردي والفيروزيِّ ولونِ البحيرةِ الأزرقِ، تِلكَ البحيرةِ التي كانتْ تعيشُ فيها سمكتُهَا. وكانتْ يِهْ – شِنْ تحتذي في قدميْهَا حذاءً ذهبيًا. ذهبتْ يِهْ – شِنْ برشاقةٍ كالصَّفصافَةِ المُتمايِلَة مع الرِّيحِ.

Once her stepmother and stepsister were out of sight, Yeh-hsien knelt before her fish bones and made her wish. It was granted in an instant.

Yeh-hsien was clothed in a robe of silk, and her cloak was crafted from kingfisher feathers. Each feather was dazzling bright. And as Yeh-hsien moved this way and that, each shimmered through every shade of blue imaginable – indigo, lapis, turquoise, and the sun-sparkled blue of the pond where her fish had lived. On her feet were shoes of gold. Looking as graceful as the willow that sways with the wind, Yeh-hsien slipped away.

ما أن اقتربَتْ يِهْ – شِنْ مِنْ مكانِ المهرجانِ حتى أَحَسَّتْ بالأرضِ ترتجُّ بإيقاعِ الرقصِ. وأخذَتْ تَشُمُّ
رائحةَ اللحْمِ الطريِّ المشويِّ والنبيذِ الدافِئِ المُبَهَّرِ. سمعَتْ أنغامَ الموسيقى وأصواتِ الغناءِ والضحكِ.
وحيثُمَا نظرَتْ رأَتْ أُناسًا يُمضونَ وقْتًا مُمْتِعًا. ابتسمَتْ يِهْ – شِنْ ابتسامةً عريضةً كلُّها فرَحٌ.

As she approached the festival, Yeh-hsien felt the ground tremble with the rhythm of dancing. She could
smell tender meats sizzling and warm spiced wine. She could hear music, singing, laughter. And everywhere
she looked people were having a wonderful time. Yeh-hsien beamed with joy.

أَخَذَت الرُؤوسُ تَلْتَفِتُ نحوَ الفتاةِ الغريبةِ الرائعةِ الجمالِ.

تساءَلَتْ زَوْجَةُ الأبِ "مَنْ هذهِ الفتاةُ؟" وهيَ تُحَدِّقُ بِيهْ – شِنْ.

أَجَابَتِ ابْنَتُهَا مُكَشِّرَةً مُتَسَائِلَةً: "إنَّها تُشبِهُ يِهْ – شِنْ بَعْضَ الشَّيْءِ."

Many heads turned towards the beautiful stranger.
"Who *is* that girl?" wondered the stepmother, peering at Yeh-hsien.
"She looks a little like Yeh-hsien," said the stepsister, with a puzzled frown.

أَحَسَّتْ يِهْ – شِنْ بِقُوَّةِ تحديقِهِمَا فالتَفَتَتْ وَوَجَدَتْ نفسَهَا وجهًا لوجهٍ مع زوجةِ أبيهَا. جَمُدَ قلبُها واختفَتْ ابتسامَتُها. فرَّتْ يِهْ – شِنْ بِسرعةٍ كبيرةٍ فانزَلَقَ حذاءُهَا مِنْ رِجْلِها. لكِنَّهَا لَمْ تَجْسُرْ أَن تَلْتَقِطَهُ فركضَتْ نحوَ البيتِ حافيةَ القدمينِ.

Yeh-hsien felt the force of their stares and turned around, and found herself face to face with her stepmother. Her heart froze and her smile fell. Yeh-hsien fled in such a hurry that one of her shoes slipped from her foot. But she dared not stop to pick it up, and she ran all the way home with one foot bare.

عندمَا عادتْ زوجةُ أبيهَا إلى البيت وجدَتْ يهْ – شِنْ نائِمةً تعانقُ إحدَى أشجارِ الحديقة. حدَّقَتْ بابنةِ زوجِهَا لمدَّةٍ طويلةٍ ثُمَّ ضحكَتْ ضحْكَةً تُشبهُ الشَّخيرَ.

تهكمت زوْجَةُ الأب: "ها، كيفَ كانَ بإمْكاني أنْ أظُنَّ انكِ *أنتِ* المرأةُ التي كانتْ في المهرجانِ؟ هذه سخافةٌ مِنيّ!" ولَمْ تعُدْ تُفكِّرُ في الموضوعِ بعدُ.

ماذا حصلَ للحذاءِ الذهبيِّ؟
بَقِيَ مخبئًا بينَ الأعشابِ الطويلةِ، تَغسلُهُ الأمطارُ وتعلوهُ قطراتُ النَدَى.

When the stepmother returned home, she found Yeh-hsien asleep, with her arms around one of the trees in the garden. For some time she stared at her stepdaughter, then she gave a snort of laughter. "Huh! How could I ever have imagined *you* were the woman at the festival? Ridiculous!" So she thought no more about it.

And what had happened to the golden shoe? It lay hidden in the long grass, washed by rain and beaded by dew.

ذاتَ صباحٍ كانَ شابٌ يمشي في الضباب، لَفَت نظرَهُ لمعانُ الذَّهبِ.

تساءلَ بتلهُفٍ ويرفعُ الحذاءَ: "ما هذا؟ ... إنَّهُ لَشيءٌ مميزٌ."

أخذَ الرجلُ الحذاءَ إلى الجزيرةِ المجاورةِ التي كانَتْ تُدعَى تُوهانْ وقدَّمَها إلى المَلكِ.

قالَ المَلكُ بإعجابٍ وهو يُقَلِّبُ الحذاءَ بينَ يديْهِ: "هذا الحذاءُ فاتنٌ. إنْ أمكَنَني اللقاءُ بالامرأةِ التي يُناسِبُ هذا الحذاءُ قدمَهَا، أكونُ قَدْ عثرْتُ على زوجَةٍ لي."

أمرَ المَلكُ جميعَ نساءِ القَصرِ أنْ يَقِسْنَ الحذاءَ، لَكنَّهُ كانَ أصغرَ بأصبعٍ واحدٍ مِنْ أصغَرِ الأقْدَامِ.

قالَ المَلكُ قاطِعاً على نَفسه عَهدًا: "سأُفَتِّشُ المَمْلَكَةَ كُلَها." لكنْ لَمْ توجَدْ قدمٌ واحدةٌ بقياسِ الحذاءِ.

أعْلَنَ المَلكُ: "يجبُ أَن أَعثُرَ على الإمرأَةِ التي يُناسِبهَا هذا الحذاءُ، لكنْ كيفَ؟"

أخيرًا خطَرت لَهُ فكرةٌ.

In the morning, a young man strolled through the mist. The glitter of gold caught his eye. "What's this?" he gasped, picking up the shoe, "…something special." The man took the shoe to the neighbouring island, To'han, and presented it to the king.

"This slipper is exquisite," marvelled the king, turning it over in his hands. "If I can find the woman who fits such a shoe, I will have found a wife." The king ordered all the women in his household to try on the shoe, but it was an inch too small for even the smallest foot. "I'll search the whole kingdom," he vowed. But not one foot fitted. "I must find the woman who fits this shoe," the king declared. "But how?"
At last an idea came to him.

وضعَ الملكُ وخدَّامُهُ الحذاءَ على جانبِ الطريقِ. ثُمَّ اختبَؤُوا يراقبونَ مَنْ يُمكنُ أَنْ يطالبَ به. عندَمَا قدِمَتْ فتاةٌ تَلبسُ ثيابًا مُمَزَّقةً وسرقتِ الحذاءَ، ظَنَّ رِجالُ الملكِ أَنَّهَا لصَّةٌ. لَكِنَّ الملِكَ كَانَ يُحَدِّقُ بِقَدَمَيهَا، فأَمَرَ رِجَالَهُ بهدوءٍ: "اتبَعُوهَا."

صاحَ رجالُ الملكِ وهُم يَقرعونَ على بابِ يِهْ – شِنْ: "اِفتَح البابَ!"
فَتَّشَ الملكُ غُرَفَ البيتِ الخلفيَّةِ فوجَدَ يِهْ – شِنْ تَحْمِلُ الحذاءَ الذَّهبيَّ بيدِهَا.
قالَ الملكُ: "مِن فضلِكِ، اِلبسيهِ."

The king and his servants placed the shoe by the wayside. Then they hid and watched to see if anyone would come to claim it.
When a ragged girl stole away with the shoe the king's men thought her a thief.
But the king was staring at her feet.
"Follow her," he said quietly.

"Open up!" the king's men hollered as they hammered at Yeh-hsien's door.
The king searched the innermost rooms, and found Yeh-hsien.
In her hand was the golden shoe.
"Please," said the king, "put it on."

وقفت زَوْجَةُ الأبِ وابنتُها بفميْهِمَا مفتوحيْنِ وهما تراقبانِ يهْ – شنْ تَذهبُ إلى مخبئتِهَا وتَعودُ لابسةً مِعطفَ الريشِ وحذاءَيْهَا الذَّهبيَّيْنِ. بَدَتْ جميلةً مِثلَ الكائنَاتِ السَّماويَّة. فَعَلِمَ الملكُ أنَّهُ قد وَجَدَ حبيبتَهُ.

وهكذا تَزَوَّجَتْ يهْ – شنْ الملكَ. فكانتِ الفوانيسُ والراياتُ والأجراسُ والطبولُ وَأشهىَ الأطعِمةَ البالِغةِ الطيبِ. ودامتِ الاحتفالاتُ سبعةَ أيامٍ.

The stepmother and stepsister watched with mouths agape as Yeh-hsien went to her hiding place. She returned wearing her cloak of feathers and both her golden shoes. She was as beautiful as a heavenly being. And the king knew that he had found his love.

And so Yeh-hsien married the king. There were lanterns and banners, gongs and drums, and the most delicious delicacies.
The celebrations lasted for seven days.

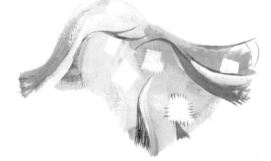

وصَارَ لِــ يِهْ - شِنْ ومَلِكُها كُلُّ ما كانا يَتَمَنَّيَاهُ. وفي ليلَةٍ منَ الليالي دَفَنَا حَسَكَ السَّمَكَةِ على شاطِئِ البحرِ حيثُ أخذَهَا المَدُّ والجَزْرُ.

أصبحَتْ روحُ السَّمَكَةِ حُرَّةً تَسْبَحُ إلى الأبدِ في البحارِ المُتَأَلِّقَةِ تَحْتَ أَشِعَّةِ الشَّمْسِ.

Yeh-hsien and her king had everything they could possibly wish for. One night they buried the fish bones down by the sea-shore where they were washed away by the tide.

The spirit of the fish was free: to swim in sun-sparkled seas forever.